THE SUN PLAYED HIDE-AND-SEEK

A PERSONIFICATION STORY

BRIAN P. CLEARY

ILLUSTRATED BY CAROL CRIMMINS

xz
c

PERSONIFICATION

M MILLBROOK PRESS/MINNEAPOLIS

To Phyllis Porter—
A Terrific Teacher
—B.P.C.

For my family
—C.C.

Text copyright © 2018 by Brian P. Cleary
Illustrations copyright © 2018 by Carol Crimmins

Millbrook Press
A division of Lerner Publishing Group, Inc.
241 First Avenue North
Minneapolis, MN 55401 USA

For reading levels and more information, look up this title at
www.lernerbooks.com.

Designed by Emily Harris.
Main body text set in Sunflower 15/18. Typeface provided by Chank.
The illustrations in this book were created with mixed media,
including graphite, ink, collage, stencils, and stamps.

Library of Congress Cataloging-in-Publication Data

Names: Cleary, Brian P., 1959- author. | Crimmins, Carol, illustrator.
Title: The sun played hide-and-seek : a personification story / Brian P.
    Cleary ; illustrated by Carol Crimmins.
Description: Minneapolis : Millbrook Press, [2018] | Summary: Rhyming
    verse demonstrating how objects can come alive when they are
    described using human traits.
Identifiers: LCCN 2016053841 (print) | LCCN 2017013723 (ebook)
    | ISBN 9781512428360 (eb pdf) | ISBN 9781467726481 (lb : alk.
    paper)
Subjects: | CYAC: Stories in rhyme. | Figures of speech—Fiction.
Classification: LCC PZ8.3.C555 (ebook) | LCC PZ8.3.C555 Su 2018
    (print) | DDC [Fic]—dc23

LC record available at https://lccn.loc.gov/2016053841

Manufactured in the United States of America
1-35339-15253-3/16/2017

There's something I've been dreading since the second week of school
when Mrs. Truman gave us each a task:
assigning us a topic that we'd research on our own
and then take turns presenting to the class.

Amber D. got similes and Angelo got puns,

while I've been asked to give a presentation

on something that gives human traits to stuff that isn't people;
my teacher calls it per-son-if-i-ca-tion.

That "stuff" could be a garbage truck, December, or the wind—
a noun that has no heartbeat, eyes, or mouth.

It compares what something does to things that people do, like, "Angry storms are marching through the South."

"How can I explain this so my classmates understand?
I need some time to stop and think," I sighed.

After school, I climbed a hill

and spied a wooden bridge,

which led me to a park called Riverside.

There, it seemed my worries packed their bags and walked away,
as I watched the sunlight tiptoe 'cross the spring.

The daffodils? They waltzed in place and kept a steady time, then leaned in close to hear the rapids sing.

A twisted oak tree beckoned me and offered up a sigh
when first I heaved myself up on its limb.

A calming breeze was whispering a whooshy little tune
as if it were a lullaby or hymn.

Across from me, a stone wall dressed in ivy stood in place.

In a crooked crack, there bloomed a single posy.

The sun and clouds played hide-and-seek against the light blue sky.

The leaves met up for ring-around-the-rosy.

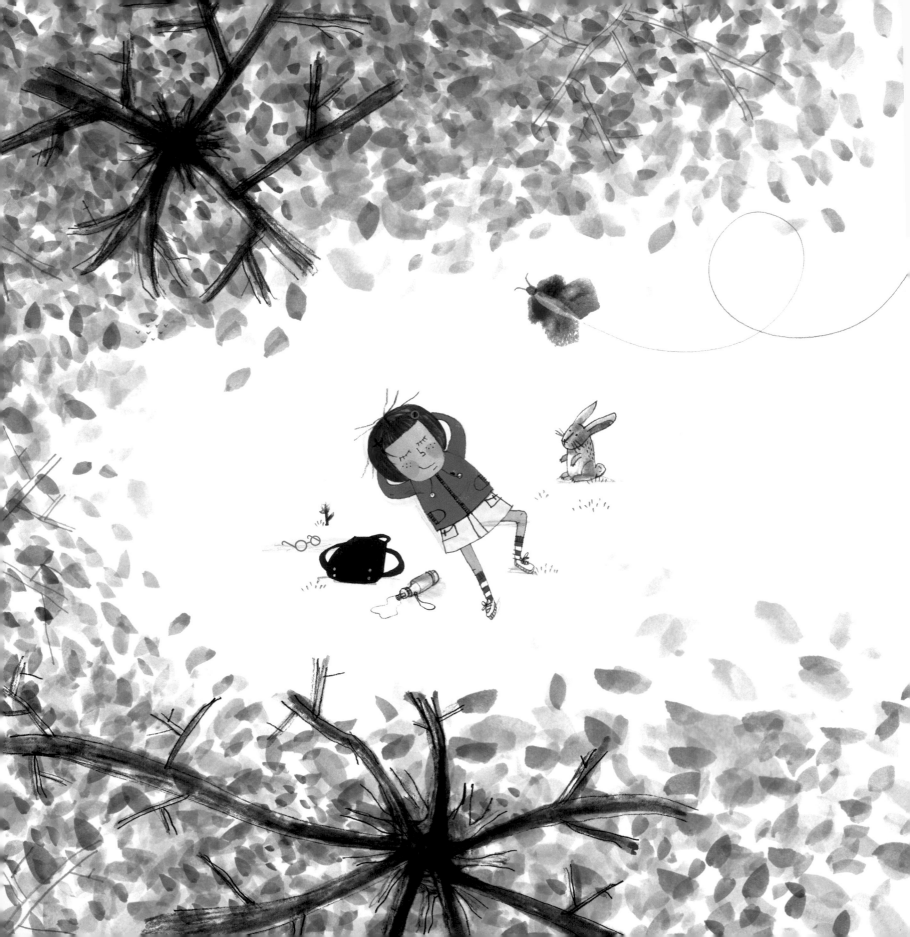

The park had been so welcoming, I nearly had forgotten
about the talk I'm giving to my class.

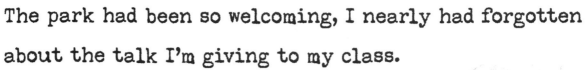

Across the way, a riding mower coughed,

then started up

and hummed across a distant bank of grass.

Sleep and rest abandoned me the night before my speech.
My mattress tossed and flipped me like a dime.

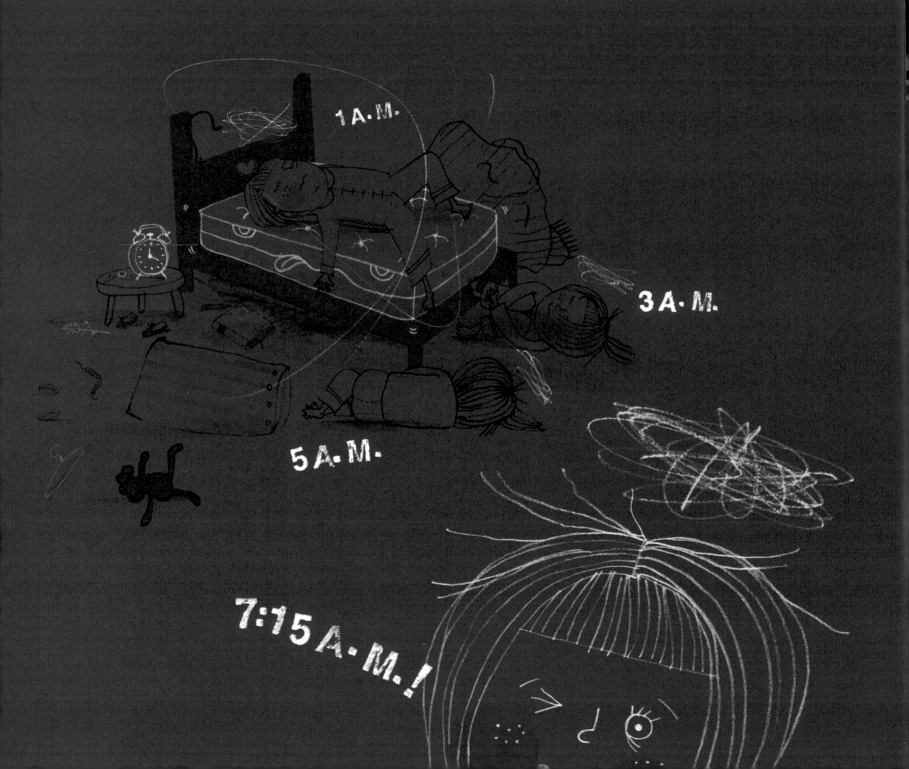

The sun awakened early, and I dressed and left for school.

The bus wheezed to a stop, and in I climbed.

WHEEE

It's presentation time at school. I'm dry-mouthed, and I'm shaky.

As I croak one single word, my heart is pounding.

Personification...

"Personification," is the only thing I say

before I hear the fire bell is sounding.

FIRE

Could I be simply dreaming this? It seems to be for real, as my classmates rise and form a single line.

I join them as we exit to the blacktop parking lot
and our spot out by the Buses Only sign.

THIS IS A
FIRE
DRILL!

BUSES
ONLY

The sunshine's warmth invites me to calm myself and breathe.

When I see the park, I say to Mrs. Truman,

"How about a field trip, so I can show the class

the way some things can be described as human?"

Not a minute later, as we're ushered by the bridge
to the park where waves are lapping at the shore,

Kayla says, "This birch tree here has shed its coat of white."

And my classmates all around me add some more . . .

"That bench is calling out my name."

"The water fountain hiccuped."

HIC!

"A beard of moss is growing on this tree."

A smile creeps across my face as Mrs. Truman beams.

The park has saved the day and rescued me!

MORE ABOUT PERSONIFICATION

Personification is a type of description that gives human traits to nonhuman things. It helps to make writing more interesting and relatable. It can also convey emotion.

You can describe the sun shining in many ways. Maybe the sun is smiling down on the world. Or maybe, instead, it's glaring. How does the personification of the sun change the mood of the sentence?

Here are some more examples of personification:

The clouds began to cry.

The dice danced down the table.

The sunflowers kissed the sky.

The wind hummed its mournful tune.

The watercooler hiccuped.

The thunder roared.

The vending machine ate my last dollar.

After I kicked it, the soccer ball leaped into the air.

The video game was begging to be played.

The soda can burped a fizzy spray.

The winter wind bit at my skin.

I woke up to the alarm clock screaming at me.

The picture jumped off the page.